MOM'S MAGIC

A PERFECT TOOL TO ACHIEVE YOUR GOAL

MOHAMMED GOUSE PASHA

Copyright © Mohammed Gouse Pasha
All Rights Reserved.

ISBN 978-1-64899-168-4

This book has been published with all efforts taken to make the material error-free after the consent of the author. However, the author and the publisher do not assume and hereby disclaim any liability to any party for any loss, damage, or disruption caused by errors or omissions, whether such errors or omissions result from negligence, accident, or any other cause.

While every effort has been made to avoid any mistake or omission, this publication is being sold on the condition and understanding that neither the author nor the publishers or printers would be liable in any manner to any person by reason of any mistake or omission in this publication or for any action taken or omitted to be taken or advice rendered or accepted on the basis of this work. For any defect in printing or binding the publishers will be liable only to replace the defective copy by another copy of this work then available.

This book is dedicated to my mother. And I'm very thankful to my sister and my friends to help me in completing this book. And I'm suggesting to every parent or guardian to read this book and make good habits and behavior in their children.

Contents

Foreword — *vii*

Preface — *ix*

Acknowledgements — *xi*

Prologue — *xiii*

1. Success — 1
2. Power Of Words — 8
3. Perfect Practice — 13
4. Purpose Of Human Life — 15
5. Opportunity — 18
6. Secret Of Winning — 20
7. Future Thoughts — 23
8. Selection Of Choice — 27
9. Problems In Life — 29
10. Purpose Of Choosing Aim — 32

Epilogue — 35

Conclusion — 37

Extra Phrases — 39

Foreword

Dear parents,

    please Don't mind my words, but try to understand. if your child is in a teenage, then please give him/her a little bit of privacy. If your children have huge no.of friends then try to understand their feelings towards their friendship. if your son has friendship with any girl, it doesn't mean he has any affection or relation or any attraction. They are just true friends. Please don't misunderstand their friendship. Maybe you are scaring about their future, they are teenagers. they know what to do. If they did any mistake, support them to make out corrections in that. if your child is feeling uncomfortable then leave him/her alone. Because they want to do something which is related to their future, but they won't allow you to watch, when it will be successful they only bring it to you. Teenage is only the period where they will decide that, what should they have to do in their life. Don't decide their future in your way. Give them a chance to make a own decision. Give them a freedom to build their own future. As parents we only have to encourage them towards their future. As a parent, we can give any suggestion but we can't take any decision in their personal life.

    If you suspected of your child it means that you insulting on nature which you had given to them in their childhood. kindly requesting you to please don't suspect your children. Give them their own freedom, and make them live as a Lion in the Jungle not as the Lion in the Circus.

Preface

Success does not mean an absence of problems. Success is not measured by how high we go up in life, but how many times we bounce back when we fall down.

But this book gives you a habit and inspiration which are given by a mother to her children for success in their life. Have you ever wondered why some people are more successful than others? It is no secret; they simply think and act in a different manner. Successful people accept responsibility, through which they can prove themselves.

This book shows you to live a life with meaningful and it will help to motivate ourselves to reach our goal. This book is written in the manner of Phrases and a story that will give you a brief meaning and explanation of that phrase, which will inspire you to achieve your Goal.

Acknowledgements

I very thankful to the Notion Publishers to bring me this golden opportunity to publish my book and to serve.

Actually, I'm very interested in writing phrases and I thought that I just finish up to phrases only. But suddenly I start writing a story on my 1st phrase. Slowly I tried to frame new stories and starts searching famous personalities whose biography was never read anywhere. I'm very poor at Grammer also, but I took help from my friend "Vinayak" and the Internet to make the proper correction. This book gave me a very new experience in my life that I never met.

But now I'm trying to make some articles and write a book on an autobiography.

Prologue

Success is a game; the more times you play the more times you win and more times you win then more successfully you will play.

As I already told you that this book is full of Phrases and meaningful stories that help you to understand the exact meaning of that phrase. If you don't understand the moral of the story then once again go through the same story. Then you will get an explanation more than when you read previous time. I kindly requesting you to please follow the habits which I wrote In this book.

All the Best

CHAPTER ONE

SUCCESS

There Is No Magic Wand for Succ

ess. In the Real World, Success Comes to Doers Not to Observers.

I will introduce a Great personality which is suitable for the above Phrase. A girl who completed her secondary education at the age of 8, completed her Intermediate at the age of 10, graduated from St. Mary's College at the age of 13, Completed her Post Graduation from Osmania University and now she pursuing her Ph.D. She is the Youngest Post Graduate from Asia. She is non-other Than a Youngest Girl NAINA JAISWAL.

She was born on 22nd March 2000 in Hyderabad. She was not only good at studies but also, she is a Master Player in Table Tennis. She won multiple titles in both National and International Championships.

I introduce one more great Personality who Known for Youngest Girl in the world to scale Mount EVEREST at the age of 14.

She is none other than POORNA MALAVATH. Poorna was born on 10th JUNE 2000 at Pakala village, Nizamabad district of Telangana State. She joined the Telangana Social Welfare Residential Educational institutions society for her education. Her talent was spotted by the Secretary of the society Dr. R. S. Praveen Kumar(IPS). She was shortlisted for Operation Everest Along with Sadhanapalli Anand Kumar. In operation for climbing, she trekked to the mountains of Ladakh and Darjeeling. After so much hard work and due to her struggle, she achieved this position.

So, friends, there are so many people who are want to achieve their personal goal but they can't achieve it. So, don't try to just watch, try to do your best for your goal. No one will tell you to do all the things, you only have to decide whatever you can.

I introduce one more mountain climber, she also made a record in climbing the Mt. Everest but a small difference is she doesn't have her left leg. But she doesn't care about anything, she just wants to made a such type of amazement in this world. She is non other than **Ms. Arunima Sinha.**

Sinha was born in Ambedkar Nagar near Lucknow in Uttar Pradesh. Her father was an engineer in Indian Army and her mother was a supervisor in health department. She had an elder sister and a younger brother. Her father died when she was 3 and her sister's husband started to take care of her family.

Before mountaineer she was like to do Cycling, and she was a football player and national Volley Ball player. She wants to join Paramilitary forces. Finally, she got a call letter from CISF (Central Industrial Security Force). But suddenly a single Incident changed her life. When she was going for CISF selections some robbers are attacked her. They robbed all the things and pushed out from Train. Recounting the incident, she said "I resisted and they pushed me out of the train. I could not move. I remember seeing a train coming towards me. I tried getting up. By then, the train had run over my leg. I don't remember anything after that". Immediately, as she fell on the railway track, another train on a parallel track crushed her leg below the knee. She was rushed to the hospital with serious leg and pelvic injuries, and lost her leg after doctors amputated it to save her life.

Due to her service for India as a national Player, she was offered compensation of ?25,000 by the Indian Sports Ministry. the Minister of State for Youth Affairs and Sports **Ajay Maken** announced an additional Rs. ?200,000 compensation as medical relief, together with a recommendation for a job in the CISF. Indian Railways also offered her a job

On 18 April 2011, she was brought to the All India Institute of Medical Sciences for further treatment, spending four months at the Institute. She was provided a Prosthetic leg free of cost by a private Delhi-based Indian company.

After few days, an inquiry by the police into the incident threw her version of the accident into doubt. According to the police, she was either attempting suicide or met with an accident while crossing the railway tracks. Arunima claimed that the police were lying. Contrary to the police claims the Lucknow bench of Allahabad high court ordered Indian Railways to pay a compensation of ₹500,000 to Arunima Sinha.

She was not satisfied with all those compensations. She wants to do something different through which she can prove herself as she doesn't need any compensation or mercy or sympathy. So, for that, while still being treated in the All India Institute of Medical Sciences, she resolved to climb Mount Everest. She was inspired by cricketer Yuvraj Singh (who had successfully battled cancer) and other television shows, "to do something" with her life. She excelled in the basic mountaineering course from the Nehru Institute of Mountaineering, Uttarkashi, and was encouraged by her elder brother Omprakash to climb Everest. She climbed Mt Everest with a prosthetic leg, which was arranged by raising funds with the help of a swami of Ramakrishna Mission, Vadodara.

She contacted Bachendri Pal, the first Indian woman to climb Mount Everest. In 2011 by telephone and signed up for training under her at the Uttarkashi camp of the Tata Steel Adventure Foundation (TSAF) 2012.

Sinha climbed Island Peak (6150 metres) in 2012 as preparation for her ascent of Everest

Sinha and Susan Mahout, a USAF (United states Air Force) instructor, who had together climbed Mount Chaser

Sangria (6,622 meters or 21,726 feet) in 2012 under the guidance of Hendrick Pal started their ascent of Mount Everest. After a hard toil of 17 hours, Sinha reached the summit of Mount Everest at 10:55 AM on 21 May 2013, as part of the Tata Group-sponsored Eco Everest Expedition, becoming the first female amputee to scale Everest. She took 52 days to reach the summit. She wrote a small message thanking the Almighty on a wrapped cloth and pressed it in the snow, "It was my tribute to Shankara Bhagawan, and Swami Vivekananda who has been an inspiration throughout my life".

After the climb, Uttar Pradesh then-incumbent chief minister **Akhilesh Yadav** honoured Arunima sinha and handed over two cheques for an amount of Rs. 25 lakhs in a function organised at her residence in Lucknow. The cheques included of Rs. 20 lakhs from the state government and a cheque of Rs. 5 crores on behalf of the Samajwadi Party. Chief minister said "Sinha by her hard work and determination had climbed the Mount Everest and created history". She was congratulated by the Indian Sports Minister Jitendra Singh on her achievement.

Arunima Sinha is now dedicated towards social welfare and wants to open a free sports academy for the poor and differently abled people. She is donating all the financial aids getting through awards and seminars for the same cause. The academy would be named **Shaheed Chandra Shekhar Vikalang Khel** Academy.

She wrote the book "Born again on the mountain", launched by Prime minister of India Narendra Modi in December 2014.

Then After She was awarded with Padma Shri, the fourth highest civilian award of India, in 2015. She was Awarded Tenzing Norgay Highest Mountaineering Award in India same as Arjun Award.

After climbing the Mt. Everest Arunima Sinha's next goal was to climb all the seven highest peaks in all seven continents. She covered six peaks, i.e. in Asia, Europe, South America, Australia, Africa and North America by 2014. She summited Mt. Elburs of Russia (Europe) Elevation 5,642 m (18,510 ft), Prominence 4,741 m (15,554 ft) and Kilimanjaro of Tanzania (Africa)Elevation 5,895 m (19,341 ft) and Prominence 5,885 m (19,308 ft). On

4January 2019, she climbed the seventh peak on Antarctica and became world's first female amputee to climb Mount Vinson.

As girls they did this type of huge things in their life. They just want to prove themselves. And they got so many difficulties and problems. But they won't count any of them. They just want to make real what they want. If we talk about these types of personalities there are so many persons.

I introduce one more personality, who started his business at a young age only. he is none other than Mr. Tilak Mehta from Mumbai, who launched a company Papers N Parcels in2018, to ease courier services in Mumbai. We all know that Mumbai is the fastest moving city in India and how much struggle we have to put to grow in such type of city. But a small boy did it and shown to us that "there is no magic wand to get success, just we have to think out of the box and make our self-develop".

Now he is studying his secondary education from "Garodia International Centre for Learning" in Mumbai.

His company is the same as "Dabbawala". But it supplies only Lunch Boxes. Whereas PNP supplies Papers and any kind of parcel from one place to another place in Mumbai.

the main reason to start his business is "one day he was stuck in a situation in which he was helpless. He had forgotten his books at his uncle's place when he was in the 7th standard. He wanted those to be delivered the same day to his place. Since his exams were approaching. He couldn't find any way to do that. Some delivery companies are charging from Rs250-300. This made him wonder how people who don't have peons or drivers manage to get their stuff delivered within the city. So, he thought, why not have a company to facilitate same-day delivered within the city?". Then he sold his idea to a banker and convinced him to resign his job and join him as the Chief Executive, and also roped in the famed Dabbawalas of the city to help with the last-mile distribution.

So, friends don't be scared of anything. Do whatever you can. Remember that, Fear is the 1st step to your failure. So be brave and be honest.

CHAPTER TWO

POWER OF WORDS

Dropping the Words Is Easy, But We Can't Retrieve Them Back. So, We Have to Be Careful While Choosing Words.

There are two friends, one is Johnny and the other is Tony. Johnny is a Manager of a big company. He just always thinks about his job and his prestige. One day his friend (Tony) met him in his company. He asked for a small job. Johnny offered him as a Team leader based on his experience when they were studying in college. Both were happy. After few days Johnny assigned him a project which he has to complete in 4 months. Tony completed his project within the time and he submitted also it. Tony trying to inform about his completion of the project but Johnny was busy in his duty and he won't listen to any word of his friend. Tony was on leave for 20 days because his mom was suffering from a kind of disease. When the submission time came Tony was absent. Johnny was so angry with him and talk to him in vulgar language and even he forgets that Tony is his friend. But Tony was listening to his words silently & he just simply resigned his job. Then after a few hours, he just checked his files which are in the desk of the table & saw a new file which has details about Tony's project and a letter which was written by him.

In the letter, Tony wrote as,

Dear Johnny,

Thanks for giving me this wonderful job. Even not only a job you gave me a life with wonderful colors. I can't pay back anything to you because there is no anything through which can I do. I just follow your rules and make you always happy. That file belongs to the project with 100% success which you have given to me and I submitted that file before 20 days because I will be in the hospital at the time of submission. Please don't mind. I just accept my project.

Yours Lovingly

Tony.

When Johnny read that letter, he felt guilty and went to Tony's home & ask him to forgive. But Tony doesn't hear a single word of him. He just asks him to go away.

But Johnny asked so many times to forgive his mistake and said: "I took back my words which I told". Then Tony wants to do a small favor for him. Johnny was ready for everything. Tony said, take a small sack full of Feathers and through them in-ground or in an empty area where there is full air. Johnny did that task. Again, Tony asks him to recollect all those feathers which he has thrown in-ground (which was highly impossible). Johnny said that I can't recollect them. Tony said, "your words are also like that only, once you have thrown then you can't get them back again".

So, friends be careful while talking Because one word can change your entire life, which is already you made and making.

Some people are trying to help people in form of suggestions. That is good, but not in all the time. For example, some students collecting funds in their college to help someone, a person (student/staff) came to them and giving his suggestions. But students are not ready to listen to his suggestions at that time. Because they want to complete their task as soon as possible, and they think like, this person is wasting our time. But they can't express their feelings. And doing like that was also not a good thing. But we can give our suggestions in proper time like, "just tell them after completion of your task come to me, I will give my suggestion, maybe it will help you in your task". In this way, we can help anyone in any type of situation.

One more thing friend, most of our friends are being some times in some kind of trouble and they ask us for help. But we scold them, beat them and do some useless arguments. But that is helpless, useless, and worthless. On another hand They think like "I'm already in a problem and now this is one bigger problem" and they won't take any help from you. But as a friend, we want to help them. Then your 1st tries to bring out them from that problem, then after do whatever you want.

We should have to always help full for our friends not as a problem in another problem. If you can't help, then directly tell them "sorry friend I can't help you". At least they can able to search for another source instead of depending on you. So please try to do whatever you can for the people who are in problems. and remember one thing, I tell you in Hindi *"**Apne liye dua karo tho jannath milthi hai, par apnon ke liye dua karo tho jannath banane vaala miltha hai.**"* It means that *"**if you pray for your self then you get Heaven. But If you pray for ourselves then you get owner of Heaven**"*. Decide yourself, which one you need, a single home or owner of all homes

MOM'S MAGIC

CHAPTER THREE

Perfect Practice

Don't Do Practice to Become Perfect, Do Perfect Practice to Become Perfect.

An Athlete doing practice daily for his game. He practiced a lot as much who never did that type of practice. He makes no. of rounds on track, but he becomes so tiered after his practice. He has a sports event in which he has to win. (Obviously, everyone wants to win) but it is very important to him. For that event, he practiced a regular manner. But he loses the race because of his practice. He just runs on the track but not in a proper manner. His total practice becomes worthless to his event. After knowing about his way of practicing one coach came to him and ask to join his academy. Without any queries, the athlete joined his academy. When his practice was started his coach was shocked at his dedication towards practice. Then coach was decided that

"I have to make him as Champion". Then the practice was started under the coach in a proper manner. As per coach guidelines, athlete follows them and made his practice as his success.

So, friends do the perfect practice. In nowadays everyone blaming themselves as "my practice is totally worthless". But the truth is they don't follow the proper and perfect way in which they have to do the practice. That's why they don't any good results. Only the difference between Practice and Perfectpractice should be "perfect". Remember this word and the way which you have chosen

CHAPTER FOUR

PURPOSE OF HUMAN LIFE

Our Happiness Is Lies in The Happiness of Our Other People. Give Them Their Happiness, You Will Get Your Happiness. And This Is the Purpose of Human Life.

The best people in our life are our parents. If you won't be happy then first make your parents happy. Because, they only the ones who need your success, who needs you to be in a good position.

But nowadays most of the people were so busy in their personal life. Somebody is forgotten about their parents and about their family members also. But this type of life will give any kind of happiness, it will give only problems both physical and mental.

In a small village, there is a woodcutter. He daily goes to a forest and cuts the trees and sells them in the market. He will get some money which helps to live his daily routine life. One day a businessman came to the woodcutter and ask to cut the trees and sell to him. A businessman offers a good salary and shelter to him. Immediately woodcutter joined his work and started cutting trees. On 1st day he cut the trees about 100. The businessman has appreciated him for his hard work and gave a bonus to him. Woodcutter thought that "if I work very hard daily, then I will get a daily bonus and I will become rich in a very short period". But on the 2nd day, he cut only 80 trees and hand over to businessman.

Woodcutter gets shocked because he cut only 80 trees & decided that "I will cut 120 trees by tomorrow and get extra bonus". But again, on the next day, he cut only 50 trees. Again, he was shocked and went to businessmen and said that "I'm resigning from my job. I'm not able to cut the trees, my count is decreases day by day, I will go back to my village". After hearing his words businessman get laughed and asked that "are you sharpen the tool (AXE) daily"? the woodcutter said "no sir". Then the businessman said, "if you won't sharp your tool then how will you cut the trees"? then the woodcutter accepts his blunder mistake and gets back to sharp the tool and start his work.

In the above story, Axe is our parent, family members, friends, etc. if you won't care about the sharpness(caring) of your axe (family members, etc.,) then how will you get good results and how will you be happy?So please care about themselves. Then you will be happy and they also happy.

CHAPTER FIVE

OPPORTUNITY

Don't Be Discouraged If Something Is Not in Today, Better Opportunities Are Waiting Ahead.

Let me tell you about sensational news which is happened in India recently.

A 42 year -old debt-ridden farmer "MALLIKARJUNA" was living in Chitra Durga which is 200 km away from Bengaluru in Karnataka. He has 10 acres of land. He cultivates different types of crops in his agricultural land. But from 2004 he started cultivating Onion. I don't know, what did he saw in onion but he still cultivating Onion only. He faced a lot of difficulties, debts, Losses while cultivating. He didn't give any give up while cultivating, he just continued his work. He invested about 15 lakhs to cultivate

Onion. But this time (2018) he got 5-10 lakhs of profit.

Again, he took a loan about 15 lakhs to cultivate again onion. Many farmers were not well cultivating due to some drought conditions there. But that year's journey was not easy. The period until October was stressful for him as the onion price remained low. This time (2019) he hit a jackpot. Onion price rose to 7000/- per quintal in October whereas in November it rises to 12000/- per quintal and he cultivated about 240 tones i.e., around 20 trucks load. He became rich and he clears his all debts and he built a new home for his family. He and his family members take turns to guard the crop against onion thieves.

The main thing is, we have to be with patients. Just try for what you want automatically it will come to you.

If MALLIKARJUNA has given up like other farmers then he won't become rich today. So, friends don't discourage yourself, always be positive and wait for good results.

CHAPTER SIX

Secret of winning

If We Want to Win Then We Have to Serve Our Neighbors, Our Families, Our Employees, Then We Win Automatically.

I will tell you a holistic real story which was happened before 2 years somewhere in India.

There is a 50 years old lady, who is suffering from Cancer. She is very rich. Her children also well settled in their personal life. She took the treatment at famous hospitals in well-developed countries, but no use of any type of treatment. She was reached to the critical condition of cancer, then one doctor told to their family members to "go to Dubai, there is one hospital which may cure her disease". That doctor also not sure about her complete treatment in Dubai. But she decided to go and take treatment in Dubai. But the main problem is her family members need one caretaker who took all the responsibilities of their mother's health. The period of treatment in Dubai was about 4 months, that's why no one caretaker came front to take responsibility. They offer so many good needs and money also, but no one accepts their offers.

At last one, women came & accept their offer and ready to go with them. That woman also facing some personal problems in her life i.e., she gave birth to a child and his Husband has died in an accident. She doesn't have any backup to take care of her child. That's why she accepts that offer. She just gave birth to her child and handover to his mother-in-law to take care of his health for 4 months until she won't come back from Dubai. But that family doesn't know about her problem and accepts her as a caretaker.

They went to Dubai for treatment and that women doing her work properly. In between sometimes, she faces some problems with regard to her after pregnancy. She just went into a room and locked the door and be there for 1 to 2 hours. She faces that problem twice or thrice in a week. Someday the Old woman(patient) asked her "do you have any personal problem" she said "no mam, nothing". It just continues for 1 month. After 1 month again she faces the same problem and gets into a room for 1-2 hours. But this time that old woman asked her very strictly. She replied, "I gave birth to my child in last month & my husband died in an accident, I don't have that much of money to take proper care of my child. The money which you had given to me, I just sent to my mother-in-law for caring for my child. I promise you I never repeat again, just last time excuse me.

But that old woman dismissed her from a job and sent to her village. Not only with empty hands but also, she (old woman) gave some suitable amount of money which is used to take proper care of her child. And the old woman orders her sons for sending the money every week and she took all the responsibilities of that child. (this is the way which we have to shows humanity towards people but nowadays no one cares about their neighbor or their friends. Everyone is busy in their personal life)

Do you know what happens at last with that old woman, By GOD'S Grace her cancer was totally cured. All the doctors were shocked. That is what profit for having helping nature.

So, friends help your friends, parents, neighbors, etc., don't know which help will help us in the future.

Remember these things:
- I can smile alone, but We laugh together.
- I can enjoy myself alone, but We celebrate together.

CHAPTER SEVEN

FUTURE THOUGHTS

Our Future Is Depend on Present Thoughts, Please Think Perfect.

In the present generation, children were just studying their academic subjects only and forget about other things.

But they don't know why they are studying. Some are wanting to be 1st in class and some students are just want to pass and enjoy the time. 60% of the students are studying when their parents are forcing to study and some of them have fear. No one takes seriously about their studies and future.

They don't have any clearance in their own future. They just compare themselves with others and they also want to become like others only. No one sets their goal and Aim which they have to be achieved. They just copying others.

By God's grace, there are some students who really want to achieve something, but they don't have any idea about "how to do when to do, why to do, etc.,". If you set any goal it should be smart. You should have to maintain clarity about your goal. If you don't have any idea about your goal then it is Worthless.

I tell you a funny story...

There is a man who has a goal. He daily goes to his holy place and pray to God and ask him to fulfill his dream. He prays like

"I want a big vehicle, lot of money in my hands & surrounding girls." At last, God fulfills his dream. One day morning he receives an appointment letter regards to Bus ticket collector. He gently goes to his holy place and asks god "what did I ask and what did you gave"?

then God replied very simply "oh my dear you ask me a big vehicle, money & girls. That's why I have given that job which is totally suitable for your dream".

Maybe you have doubts about his dream, how it was fulfilled. Let me explain, he got a bus ticket collector job & the bus is also a big vehicle which runs on the road, the 2nd, bus ticket collector always have hands with full of money but it doesn't belong to him. 3rd, he wants girls around him

& that bus is especially only for ladies. Hence, as per his dream, everything is fulfilled. If he maintains clarity about his dream-like "big vehicle as any big car, own money and etc. then maybe it will become true in the proper way.

I will tell you about research which was done by the Psychology department at Harvard University in Cambridge. Researchers took 100 topmost graduates from their entire university and told them to take a piece of paper and write their aim or goal which they want to achieve or reach. Researchers gave one week's time to think and to decide on what should they have to write. All the students are just neglected at thinking. They didn't think anything. After one week all the students (100) are assembled in the auditorium. As per the conditions, a piece of paper and a pen was given to them. Only 3 students have filled that piece of paper & the rest of them are not filled. I really telling you friends, if researchers give any subject related questions, then exactly they will fill no. of additional papers. But they can't fill a small piece of paper which will decide their entire life.

The research was not ended up, after 25 years researchers again start an investigation of those 100 students. The 97 people who are not filled their piece of paper, they were earning lakhs of rupees per month. (You everyone know about the jobs and salaries of the people who are studied at Harvard University). But the 3 persons who filled their piece of paper with their aims and goals, their salary was equals to 10 times greater than the sum of all those 97 students salaries. That is the power of Aiming and setting a goal for life.

If you also have dreams and don't know about the parameters which you have to follow, then your dream is worthless. So, friends Aim high and maintain clarity otherwise your situation also becomes like that bus ticket collector.

Your goal should be SMART

S- Specific

M- Measurable

A- Achievable

R- Realistic

T- Time bonding

So, friends be careful about your aim and goal.

CHAPTER EIGHT

SELECTION OF CHOICE

Select and Do for Others Which You Have Select & Do for Yourself.

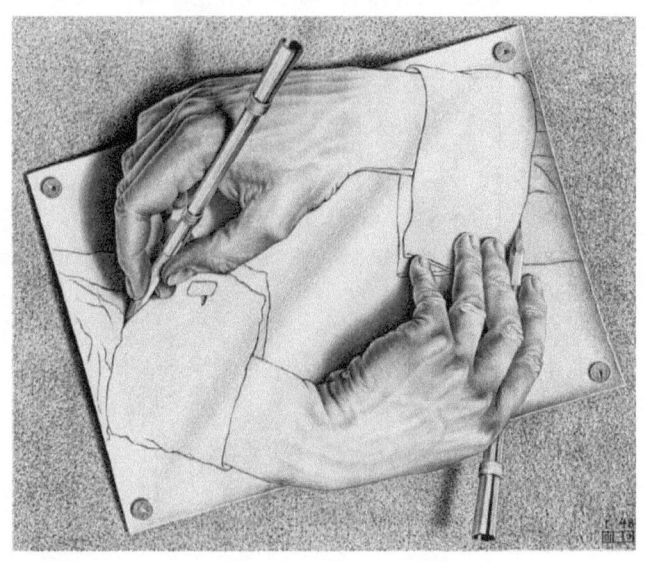

There are two friends Rohit and Mohit. They planned to start a new Real-estate Business. For that, Rohit took the responsibility of all the Tenders, and Official Agreements, whereas Mohit took all the Responsibilities regard to Constructions of Respective Fields. They continued their Partnership for a long time and they got very Good Status in their field. Mohit was always thought that due to his good designs only they got a good name. But he won't give any credit to his friend (Rohit), Even though they did Hard work in an equal manner. After few days Mohit wants Retirement. But Rohit said, "please took the last contract and made it with beautiful design with your own time".

But Mohit was not happy with that contract, he just took that and start construction. Mohit doesn't keep much interest in that contract as much as he kept on previous contracts. He just completed the project in an irregular manner and handover to Rohit. During Mohit's retirement Function Rohit Gifted him a key which belongs to that house which was made by Mohit on of end of his job life.

But there is no use of that house because he just made it without any good interior and exterior designs. Then he realized that "if I kept a little bit of interest in that house then it will be the good one among all the homes".

So, friends whenever you do anything for others, do it like for yourself.

CHAPTER NINE

PROBLEMS IN LIFE

Don't be defeat in your life, defeat your life to win in your life.

May be you know about the person who won 3 Gold Medals in the 1960 Rome Olympics after long struggle and she spent her total life only for running, she was none other than VILMA RUDOLF. You will amaze if you know about herself.

Vilma born in 1940 in the U.S.A. her parents have 12 children in their family. Vilma was the 10th child to her parents. At the age of 4, she was suffering from Polio disease. We all know about polio disease. Due to the polio effect, her one leg was injured and doctors said: "she can't walk now". But Vilma didn't listen to any words of them. When she looked out from windows, her brothers and sisters were running and playing. She also wants to run and play with them. Then she asked & forced her mother to buy a Shoe, through which she can able to walk. Then, at last, she was able to walk.

I think she was very lucky(actually unlucky) Because at the age of 9 she was again suffered from polio and with a bonus, she was affected by double Pneumonia and Scarlet Fever. This time she both the legs are injured. Doctors said, "there is no chance that could make her walk". This time also she didn't listen to any words of them. But this time she asked to get a shoe for her both legs. Her mom was telling to her "please don't force yourself, don't try to take the risk, otherwise it will lead to a very big problem" She took 1 hour to walk only 10 meters, finally she was made herself to walk. In this way, she practiced for a walk, but she aimed to run.

She was suffered a long time with that disease. After a lot of struggle, she was able to run. Then she met a coach YAD TEMPLE to help her to win a gold medal. But Coach said, "you can't run and it is impossible with your personality". The Vilma said, "sir I don't want to listen to any impossible word, I just want it with my Dedication". Then Coach agreed and impressed at her dedication. He prepared her well full practice and she was ready to participate in Championships. In her 1st race, she got last place. In the next match she got last but one place. In this manner, she got a Gold Medal in championships. But she said, "I want to participate in the Olympics".Then, at last, she was selected for the Melbourne Olympics in 1956. She competes in Olympics but she became Runner and the winner became *Juttahin*. In every race, she comes in second place only. But she won't give up, she practiced well and again participated in the Rome Olympics in 1960. This time was just a miracle happens. In 1956 she lost 1st place in the hands of Juttahin, then again, she competes with her only. But this time she defeats Juttahin and got 1st place. Not only in 100mts race but also 200mts & 400mts. She Participated in 100*4mts relay also. But at the time of catching the baton, she missed that and other participants were already nearer to the end line. But Velma took that baton and run like a Thunder and she defeats all the participants in Relay also. Finally, she achieved her goal and got Gold medals in running.

Friends, here Velma was not competing with others, she competes with herself and finally, she defeats herself. Because she knows that, no one defeats her, except her paralyzed life. So that's why she wants to defeat her life. If she also sat like other paralyzed people then she never got the Gold medal.

So, friends don't make any silly personal reasons for your faults. Try to make out yourself from that problem and get succeed in the work.

CHAPTER TEN

PURPOSE OF CHOOSING AIM

Don't choose the aim as which you have already done and maybe you are the best in that. But do the best for your aim which you have already chosen.

There is a person who wants to become an IAS officer. Due to his poor family background, he can't able to achieve his goal in the required time. But he fixed mentally to became an IAS officer.

In 2008 he passed the UPSC at 5th attempt with 1226 marks and he became an IAS officer in Uttarakhand then after he worked as Magistrate for Haridwar. He is none other than Mr. Addanki Sridar Babu. He is from Andhra Pradesh. He completed his graduation in Computer Science from Vignan University.

But before IAS, he already passed the UPSC but he got IPS. Then also he won't give up and tried for IAS, & at last, he reached his goal. But before IPS he worked for Reserve Bank, then before he worked as MPDO than before he worked as a Group-2 Civil servant than before he worked as an officer in a bank than before he worked as a Bank Clerk.

Look here friends, sir was already an IPS officer and he worked in so many different types of government sectors. He can compromise with that job only, But his goal is to become an IAS officer, then in anyhow finally he reached his goal.

So, friends maybe you also good at so many things, but concentrate on your goal which you have to reach and remember that your goal should be Smart.

Epilogue

Friends remember one thing "knowing yourself is the beginning of all wisdom". Don't let the fear of being alone, make you settle for something less. It is not just being alone that worries us, it's feeling alone that worried us. This is our opportunity to get to know ourselves. For example, if you want someone to fall in love with you, we have to fall in love with ourselves first. Our biggest mistakes are that we try to get to know other's interests before we know our own. We try to learn about everyone else's like a favourite color and movie before we know our own and we learn to know what makes others happy before we learn what makes ourselves happy.

So, friends 1st tries to know yourself, then after try to know about others. As we know that "Inspiration is a way of thinking and Motivation is a way of action when our thoughts change

automatically our activities also change. So first try to inspire yourself, then try to motivate.

Conclusion

Maybe this book will help you to inspire yourself. But you will get success only when you will be going to start a work. If you were waiting for the right opportunity and waiting for the correct time, then that is worthless. You only have to search for the opportunity; you only have to bring the time through which you can play your game. You only have to think out of the box.

If you really want to win in your life then follow your heart not matter what. And most of the people are telling about luck like "my luck is always bad and I'm only the unlucky person in this world" & etc. "Don't blame your luck. Because luck is what you're doing for yourself. If you are doing it properly then automatically you will get good results. Otherwise don't know what will happen."

I think I told you to remember a lot of things, but you have to do. The main motto of this book is just to inspire yourself and being a motivation to others. I believed in that "the best way of learning is sharing our knowledge with others".

Extra Phrases

Here I'm writing some extra phrases which may help you with internal motivation.

- Think only the best, work only for the best and expect only the best.
- Never compromise on two things:

1. Self-Respect
2. Integrity

- Your parents can't give what you want, but they can give definitely whatever they can. So, don't try to force them. Be happy with whatever you have.
- You can win only when you defeat yourself. Because there is no one who defeats you.
- Never forget what others have done for you,
- Never remember what you have done for others.
- Feeling good is the natural outcome of doing good, and doing good is the outcome of Being good.
- Don't think HOW I have to solve a problem; think WHY I have to solve?
- Develop a reason to live your life as to why we have to live?
- This life is a one-way street, there is no rewind button. The questions are what time is it? And where we are? Only the answer is "Time is now and we are here".
- Ability teaches how we have to do; motivation teaches why we have to and Attitude decides how well we do.
- There is no substitute for hard work. The harder you work and the luckier you get.

EXTRA PHRASES

- Everything that we are enjoys is a result of someone's hard work. Some work is visible while others go unseen, but ultimately both are equally important.
- Don't be scared to anything, be brave like everything will scare you.

www.ingramcontent.com/pod-product-compliance
Lightning Source LLC
LaVergne TN
LVHW041547060526
838200LV00037B/1183